Pucker

Ted Staunton

Illustrations by Bill Slavin

Formac Publishing Company Limited
Halifax

Formac Publishing Company Limited acknowledges the support of the
Cultural Affairs Section, Nova Scotia Department of Tourism, Culture
and Heritage. We acknowledge the financial support of the
Government of Canada through the Book Publishing Industry
Development Program (BPIDP) for our publishing activities.

We acknowledge the support of the Canada Council for the Arts for
our publishing program.

Library and Archives Canada Cataloguing in Publication

Staunton, Ted, 1956-
    Pucker up, Morgan / Ted Staunton ; illustrated by Bill Slavin.

(First novels)
ISBN 978-0-88780-746-6 (bound).--ISBN 978-0-88780-744-2 (pbk.)

    I. Slavin, Bill II. Title. III. Series.

PS8587.T334P79 2008   jC813'.54   C2007-907501-0

Formac Publishing
Company Limited
5502 Atlantic Street
Halifax, NS B3H 1G4

Distributed in the
United States by:
Orca Book Publishers
P.O. Box 468
Custer, WA U.S.A.
98240-0468

Printed and bound in Canada

Table of Contents

1

Thumbs Down

Outside, it is raining. Inside, it is indoor recess. Aldeen Hummel and I are hungry.

I know I am hungry because my tum is zapping *Feed Me, Feed Me* signals to my brain. I know Aldeen is hungry because she just grabbed Kaely's cookies and stuffed them in her mouth. Aldeen is the Godzilla of Grade Three.

"HEY! You took my cookies," Kaely yells.

"Ib bnop." Aldeen's cheeks are like balloons. Crumbs dribble out from between her lips.

"Did too!"

Aldeen's eyes squinch behind her glasses. She balls up her fists at the end of her skinny arms. She may be a string bean, but you don't mess with Godzilla.

Kaely runs out to where our teacher, Mrs. Ross, is standing in the hall. I go back to being hungry. My snack is boring carrot sticks. My best friend Charlie has chocolate-chip granola bars. I know what I'm going to do. I've been waiting all morning to do it.

"Hey, Charlie," I say. "I'll show you a

magic trick for a granola bar."

"Cool," says Charlie. That is one reason he is my best friend.

I like magic. I know two tricks. Charlie has seen those. This new one is way cooler; my dad brought it home for me last night.

"Give me the granola wrapper," I say louder. "I'll turn it into a ribbon." You're supposed to use tissues, but this should work even better.

Kids turn to watch: excellent. While Charlie peels off the shiny wrapper, I slip my hand in my pocket and stick on my new rubber thumb. It fits over my real thumb and there is a ribbon tucked inside it, squished down in the tip. I can feel it. This is so cool.

Two desks away, I see Aldeen chewing

like crazy. She swallows a monster mouthful just as Mrs. Ross gets to her. "What cookies?" I hear her ask.

Then Charlie gives me the wrapper. "Okay," I call out. "Wrapper into a ribbon."

More kids look. I wrap the wrapper around my fake thumb fast, before anyone can see much. Then I put my other hand over it. When you pull it off, see, what happens is the thumb comes off too, but everything is hidden in your hand. Then you reach in and pull out the ribbon and it looks like the wrapper has changed, like you said. Neat, huh? Then you stuff it back in, put your hand back over your thumb to put the fake back on, and give back the whole, unribboned wrapper. While everyone *ooh*s and *aah*s, you dump the rubber thumb in your pocket before they can see it. It's magic.

Except that as I pull, Aldeen yells, "THEY WERE TOO MINE!"

I jump, my hand jerks, and the rubber thumb slips right out of the silvery wrapper just as it pops off my hand. *No-o-o*. It sails

past Charlie and plops on the desk. Red ribbon hangs out.

"Oh, BOOGERS!" I yell. Everybody laughs.

"Enough yelling," says Mrs. Ross. She looks from me to Aldeen. "But thanks, you two. You've just given me an idea."

2

Not That Green

Mrs. Ross won't tell us what idea we gave her until afternoon. I am hoping the idea is that she can turn Aldeen into a pumpkin or something. Turns out, that's not it.

She tells us that our class is putting on a play for Open House night. It is called *The Frog Prince* and, because it is about magic and changing things, I get to be the star. I will be a frog, but that's okay because I like green. Also, the part has lots of talking, so it's perfect for me. Talking is one of my favourite things.

At supper I tell Mom and Dad I am the star of the school play.

"Fantastic!" Dad cheers.

"Super," says Mom. "And *The Frog Prince* is a good story. We read it, remember?"

No, I don't. What is important is I am the star. "Do I have to eat my broccoli?" I ask. Stars don't have to eat everything.

"Yes," says Dad.

Then we all clink glasses. It's a toast to me. I tell how Mrs. Ross got her idea.

"The wrapper was too slippery," Dad says. "That's why you use tissues."

I shake my head. "It was because Aldeen yelled. She wrecked it."

"What part did she get?" Mom asks. "Eat your broccoli."

"I'm eating my chicken first," I say. "She's a princess or something."

"A princess?" says Dad. "*The* Princess? There's only one in *The Frog Prince*. That's a big part too. Don't you remember? She's proud and bossy."

"That's Aldeen." Mom smiles. She kind of likes Aldeen. She lets her come over after school sometimes when Aldeen's mom and grandma are both working. "I bet she was happy to get that part," Mom says. I shrug and slide broccoli under my mashed potatoes.

"I'm full."

"Eat your broccoli," says Mom.

"Yeah," Dad says, still thinking about the play. "Remember? At the end, she — "

"Never mind," says Mom. "We'll get the book out from the library again. Right now, eat your broccoli. You just said you like green."

3

Better Magic

Two days later, we have our first practice. Mrs. Ross hasn't got the whole script written out yet, but she gives everybody the first two pages. We all move the desks away to make a space to act in.

Mrs. Ross shows Charlie and Aldeen where to stand. They start things off. Charlie is the King. He sends Aldeen the

Princess, outside to play in the castle garden and she loses her golden ball down the well. Charlie is not very kingly, but he will be better with a beard, probably.

Aldeen is not exactly princessy, either, except she is wearing a dress. She never wears dresses. Before we started she was all twitchy and loud. Now she gets red-faced and she looks at the floor. No one can hear her when she reads.

"Louder please, Aldeen," says Mrs. Ross.

She reads again. "Yes ... Father ... I ... Will ... Oh ... No ... I ... Have ... Dropped ... My ... Golden ... Ball."

Oh, yuck. She sounds like the robot in my Skateboards On Mars game.

Luckily this is where I, the Frog, come in. I go up to Aldeen.

Mrs. Ross says, "Now think, Morgan. Would a frog walk?"

Duh. I hop. Everybody yells. Duh again. I have bunny-rabbit hopped. I squat down with my hands between my knees. I hop over to Aldeen. It hurts. All that hopping does something else too. I had a long drink at the fountain at recess. Just as I get to Aldeen, I can't help it; I rip out a monster burp.

Except for Aldeen, everybody laughs, even Mrs. Ross. Aldeen jumps back as if *she's* a frog. Everybody laughs again. My face gets hot and I can't remember what I'm supposed to say. But, hey, if they laughed.... I swallow some air fast and squeeze out a mini-burp. I try to say "Ribbit" at the same time. Except for

Aldeen, everybody laughs *again*. I think I like this.

"Very good, Morgan." Mrs. Ross is still laughing. "Now say, 'Pardon, fair princess, I can get your ball for you.'"

I say it, then say "Ribbit" and sit down on the floor. My legs are killing me. There is more laughing. Aldeen looks at her pages. She is holding them so tight that they are all crumpled and she can't read them. She looks back at me, even redder in the face. Godzilla has turned into a scaredy-cat. It's magic! I think I love this.

4

Not So Funny

At our next two practices, Mrs. Ross has more pages for us. I make my voice like Kermit the Frog from *Sesame Street.* It is so funny. Aldeen still stands there and talks really slowly, so I *ribbit* while she talks. She gets all red in the face.

Charlie still isn't very kingly either, so I keep hopping and going, "Yeah, yeah,

yeah" to help. I don't get why he keeps messing up his words. He needs to practise.

Hopping makes me tired, so I switch to pretending to catch flies with my tongue. Then I smile and burp. Then it's less boring when Chantal and Tracey say their parts.

My being funny makes everything way better. Not everybody laughs, but I think that is because they are busy now. I can tell Chantal and Tracey like it, because they keep looking at me as if they are asking for help. When we stop for recess, Mrs. Ross wants to speak to me. I bet she is going to thank me for making the play so good.

Sure enough, she says, "I really like the way you are working so hard. That is an interesting voice you made up. It's a bit hard to understand, though."

"It's Kermit," I say, "from *Sesame Street*." Hasn't she ever watched it?

"Ah," says Mrs. Ross. "Ri-i-ight. You know, Morgan, maybe you're doing a bit too much. We have to give the others a chance too."

"But they don't do anything," I say. Well, they don't.

"Maybe you're not giving them time to. How about not hopping and ribbitting so much when other people are talking? Acting is teamwork, you know. Sometimes that means waiting your turn."

"Okay," I say. It doesn't matter. I can still make faces and catch flies, and I can pretend to give warts to people. Hey, I wonder if I can do my magic trick! Do frogs have thumbs?

Outside, everyone starts giggling when they see me coming. Probably they are remembering the funny stuff I did.

Charlie says, "How come your voice gets weird like that?"

"It's Kermit," I say.

"It doesn't sound like Kermit."

Yes, it does.

Then Chantal says, "Hey, Morgan, practised the *ending* yet?"

"You know how it ends, don't you?" asks Stephanie.

Kids laugh.

I don't get it. "Yeah," I say, "it ends with me getting a standing O."

"That's what you think," says Tracey.

Now they all laugh, but it doesn't sound like before.

5

The End

Now I'm worried. I have to find out the ending as soon as I get home. But when the bell rings, Aldeen is beside me. Oh, yuck. I forgot she was coming over to my house. When Aldeen comes over, she cheats at everything and hogs the snacks and I have to let her because she's the guest — and because she gives killer noogies.

Kids whisper as we leave. I walk fast. Aldeen keeps up, her witchy hair bouncing.

"You walk too fast."

"I have to do something," I tell her.

"Like what, go to the bathroom?"

"No, go to the library. You don't have to come."

"Yes, I do." She stares at me through her smudgy glasses. "You talk too fast too. You're making fun of me in the play."

Uh-oh. I look down. Her noogie finger is bent. Double uh-oh.

"No," I say. "That's to make it better. You talk too slow. You should do it like this." I say a Princess line in a princessy way. "See?"

Aldeen's mouth is open and her eyes are

big. Then they get small. "That's wussy," she says. But her noogie finger unbends. Whew; that was close.

My dad is home. He takes us to the library and we get *The Frog Prince*. Back at home we sit on the couch. Dad is in the middle. I snuggle in extra close: he's *my* dad.

Dad reads. The stuck-up Princess drops her golden ball down the well. The Frog gets it back for her because she promises to grant him three wishes. Then she changes her mind because she's too proud, but her dad the King says she has to anyway.

So the first wish is for the Frog to have supper with everyone. That's how far we are at school. The second wish is for a comfy place to sleep, so he gets the

Princess's pillow. That leaves one more wish. Dad turns to the last page. I lean forward.

Dad reads. The Frog says the Princess has to kiss him, so she does and he turns into a handsome prince. Then they get married and live happily ever after.

"Well," says Dad, "that was an interesting ending."

Nobody moves. Nobody says anything. I *can't* say anything. All I can think is, *I have to kiss Aldeen Hummel. Onstage. In front of everyone.* It is the grossest, disgustingest, unhappiest, most horrible ending I have ever heard.

Outside, a horn honks. Aldeen bounces off the couch, grabs her backpack, and zooms out the door without looking back.

6

Loose Lips

Mom and Dad say, "Don't worry; it's only acting. Everyone knows that."

Oh yeah? So next morning, why is everyone in the schoolyard chanting:

"Morgan and Aldeen
sitting in a tree
K-I-S-S-I-N-G!

First comes love, then comes marriage then comes King Kong in a baby carriage"?

Because everybody says we asked for our parts because we are secretly in love, that's why.

"It's only ACTING," I yell. "WE ARE NOT IN LOVE!"

"Oh yes, you are," they say back. "Aldeen even goes to your house!"

"I CAN'T HELP IT," I yell. "I DON'T want to kiss Aldeen, she's GROSS!" Part of my brain tells me to be careful. If Aldeen hears me say bad stuff about her, she'll pound the snot out of me. This might prove we are not in love, but still.

Everybody laughs. They go off making

smoochy noises.

"Wait," I call. They don't. I turn around and there's Aldeen. Oh-oh.

Very slowly, one finger at a time, she makes a fist, right under my nose. My bones melt. I am now a marshmallow.

Aldeen says, "Come near me, and I'll pound the snot out of you."

Godzilla is back.

7

Keep Away

For one second I think, *Whew*. Stay away from Aldeen? No problem.

Except we are together in the play. Aldeen's noogie knuckle is out all the time we practise. That afternoon I get too close, and she nails me.

"OWW!" I do a real hop, not a frog hop, away. Everybody laughs but me. After that, I stay on the other side of the stage and yell to Aldeen. Mrs. Ross sighs a lot and keeps telling us to move closer together. Aldeen won't. I can't — or I'll be mashed Morgan.

But what's going to happen when she has to kiss me? I don't want to think about it. I do more hopping and faces and fly-catching instead. Nobody laughs any more. They are probably just jealous that I am so good at acting. Besides, they are too busy making smoochy faces at me and Aldeen. Mrs. Ross tells me to tone it down. I try to, but then I forget because I start thinking about kissing again. What will Aldeen do? What will I do? *Arrgh*.

We find out the next day. Mrs. Ross gives out the last part of the script. I grab mine and read as fast as I can. Maybe we won't have to kiss. I get to the end and … It's Smooch City. I'm burnt toast. All around I hear whispers and giggles. It feels as if the whole class is watching. I look up. The whole class *is* watching.

"Let's try it," says Mrs. Ross.

My mouth is dry. I can't even ribbit. I read: "My … third wish is for a … kiss."

Charlie reads, "Princess. You. Must. Grant. The wish."

It goes quiet. Someone snickers. Mrs. Ross calls, "Sssh. Okay, Princess. Walk over and kiss him on the cheek."

Aldeen doesn't move.

"Aldeen?" says Mrs. Ross.

"No way," says Aldeen. Her face is pink.

Mrs. Ross smiles. "I understand.

Remember, it's just acting. *Pretend* to kiss."

"No way," says Aldeen.

Mrs. Ross smiles again. "Just kiss the air in front of Morgan. It will look real."

"No way," says Aldeen. "That's gross."

Mrs. Ross says we will take time out for snacks. She calls Aldeen and me over. "What are we going to do, team?" she sighs. "It's too late for a new Princess."

Finally she and Aldeen work it out. Aldeen will blow me a kiss from across the stage. We try it. The air kiss looks like sucking on a lemon. When Aldeen flaps to blow it towards me, she doesn't even lift her hand. It looks as if she is trying to wave away a fart.

Everybody laughs. Aldeen glares. The laughing stops. Good; I'm mad.

8

Me, Myself, and I

I'm mad because Hummel the Bummel is making me look stupid. I am so mad that, when we go out for recess, I don't even care about noogies. Well, maybe I care a little bit. I blast over to Aldeen, but I stop out of reach.

"Nice one, Aldeen," I say. "Way to wreck everything."

"Get lost, Morgan." Up comes her noogie knuckle.

"Oooooo, lovers' quarrel!" Tracey and Kaely skip by.

"Kissing is gross," Aldeen says, "and kissing you is double gross!"

Wha-a-at? Okay, kissing is gross, but kissing *me?* It's not like me kissing her; *that* would be gross. But I am the star and I'm funny and everybody likes me.

I yell, "Well, YOU'RE GROSS TOO! I'd never ever kiss you!"

She yells back, "YOU ALREADY SAID *THAT,* DIDN'T YOU?"

When I get home I am still so mad I start eating cookies without even asking.

"Whoa, there," says Dad, who is peeling carrots. "How about one at a time?"

I start telling him why I am mad, but my mouth is full and I dribble cookie crumbs. I stop and swallow, then tell how Aldeen won't kiss me and I look stupid.

"Gee," Dad says. "Maybe you should use a different aftershave."

He laughs. I don't.

Dad says, "Morgan, you're lucky this way. The story seemed different to me, so I went back to the library. There's another version of *The Frog Prince* — an older one with a different ending. If you want to see, the book is over there. Believe me, whatever happens, you'd like your ending better. And hey, you're still the star. No one can make you look stupid."

There is a library book on the kitchen table. I don't look in it. Who cares? I don't want something worse than even kissing, and Mrs. Ross isn't going to change the play anyway.

I am taking another cookie when it hits me. Dad is right. I hand the cookie to him.

"Have a wart," I say, in my best Kermit voice.

"Pardon?" he says.

Never mind. "Do frogs have thumbs?" I ask. I am the star. I am going to save the play. Aldeen Hummel is not going to make me look stupid. I can do things for myself.

9

Funny and Lovable

It's Open House night. We have practised three more times and I have been boring. Tonight I am going to be so funny and lovable it will not matter if Aldeen does a wave-away-a-fart kiss. Everyone will thank me after.

We have our costumes on. Charlie has a beard and a crown. Aldeen has a purple princess dress. Her hair is tied back and she has a crown too. You can hardly tell it's her except for her glasses. My costume is best. On top I wear a green garbage bag with black dots stuck on it for warts. It is split in the back to come off when I turn into a prince. Under it I have on green pants and a black shirt with a sash over my shoulder that says *PRINCE*. I also have a green toque that I pull off so Stephanie can stick a paper crown on my head. In my pocket is my fake-thumb trick, in case I need it.

I peek into the gym from behind the stage curtain and my stomach goes woogly. Lots of people are sitting there. My mom and dad are with Charlie's parents and Aldeen's mom and grandma.

Then the gym goes dark. The stage

lights come on. Tracey goes out to start. As soon as Aldeen drops her ball, I swallow some air, hop onto the stage, and do a humongous *ribbit* burp. Aldeen jumps. Everybody laughs and I feel great. I'm the star; it's going to work.

All the time everyone is saying their parts, I hop, ribbit, burp, make faces, hand out warts and do my Kermit voice. When we all have dinner, I catch flies. When I get the Princess's pillow, I snore. How funny and lovable can you get?

Every time I get funnier and more lovable, though, Aldeen's eyes squinch. Her face gets pink again and her noogie knuckle pops out.

Chantal hisses, "Cut it out!"

"Morgan-n-n-n," Charlie whispers behind his beard.

Well, too bad; they're just jealous. They should try harder. It's their fault the audience isn't laughing as much any more. I'm getting tired, but I go and hop around Aldeen as she talks. She'd never noogie me on stage; I'm too lovable.

And now we're at the third wish. I'm on a roll. I do one more hop and say, Kermit-style, "My third wish is for a kiss. Ribbit, ribbit, ribbit." Then I pucker up in a smoochy face, turn to Aldeen, open my arms, and yell, "Kiss me, kiss me, kiss me!" That isn't in the script but, like I said, I'm on a roll.

Aldeen doesn't kiss me. Instead — *Pow!* — she pounds me one, right in the stomach.

"Oof!" I land on my butt. The garbage bag splits; my frog toque pops off.

"GET LOST, YOU BOZO!" she yells. Then she stomps off.

10

The End of the End

There is total silence. Then everybody laughs and claps at once.

I stand up, holding my stomach under my *PRINCE* sash. It hurts; Aldeen is a hard puncher. The garbage bag has fallen off. Stephanie slaps the crown on my head.

Mrs. Ross shoves Aldeen back onstage beside me. Her tied-back hair has popped loose. Her crown is crooked and so are her glasses. She still has her fist ready, but she looks as if she's going to cry.

But when she comes out, everybody claps even harder. Tracey yells, "And they lived happily ever after!" No one hears. They are too busy standing up, still clapping. Now they are cheering too. It's a standing O. Mom and Dad are clapping with Charlie's parents and Aldeen's mom. Aldeen's grandma is pumping her fist in the air. *Wha-a-at?*

Mrs. Ross signals us to bow. We all do. It hurts my stomach. I also bump Aldeen. She jumps away and up pops her noogie knuckle. There is more laughing and clapping.

The gym lights come on. Grownups

come over to talk.

"Great acting," Mom says. "And a surprise ending! I couldn't understand why you were being so wild and silly, but with that ending it all made sense."

Huh? Before I can think, Aldeen's grandma crows,

"Ya got a good left, there Aldie."

Then Dad is saying to Mrs. Ross, "Cool! You put the old and new stories together."

Mrs. Ross smiles, sort of. You can tell that now it's her turn to think, Huh?

Dad explains. "The endings. In the story most of us know, the Princess kisses the frog. Morgan was worried about that one, heh, heh, heh. But in the old version of the story, the Frog bugs the Princess so much that she gets mad and throws him at a wall and he turns into the Prince." Dad turns to me. "I just never knew Morgan could be so good at bugging people." He hugs me to show he's kidding. I think.

I also think I am beginning to get it. Oh, boy. So much for funny and loveable.

Mrs. Ross says, "The ending was all Morgan and Aldeen. They're quite a team."

A *team?* Just a — I open my mouth. I look at Aldeen. She looks at me. My stomach still hurts. I close my mouth.

A newspaper guy wants to take a picture of us acting the end.

Aldeen straightens her crown. "How many times do you want me to hit him?"

The man laughs. "We'll see. Look surprised," he says to me.

I don't even have to act.

What else is Morgan up to?

Here's a look at what happens when Morgan signs up for soccer in *Great Play, Morgan!*

1

Soccer Genius

"Impossible! Impossible! Land it on the rail! Five-Oh! Go! NOOOOOO!"

Charlie wipes out his board again. Charlie has so many sports trophies it looks like he won the Olympics, but hey, you can't be good at everything. I'm better at skateboarding. Well, not skateboarding skateboarding. I stink at that. What we're

doing is video game skateboarding.

I'm a pro at that. It's better anyway —
you can eat while you're playing.

Charlie hands me the controller. As I
start my turn, he says, "Did you decide
about soccer yet?"

Oh yeah. Soccer. Charlie wants me to

sign up with him. His dad will be coaching the team. "Hang on," I say. I'm reverse grinding along the edge of a skyscraper roof. Right, right, left, down, down, hold on, up, up, upupUP! My fingers are flying. I'm flying. I can do anything. How hard can kicking a ball be, compared to this? Plus Charlie says they have freezies and snacks after every game.

"Sure," I say, "I'm gonna sign up."

"Great," says Charlie.

"Wonderful!" says my mom, looking into the family room. I face-plant into a dumpster. I have three thousand points and a new sport.

After supper, I dig a ball out of the garage and go over to the schoolyard. I figure I'd better try soccer while no one's around. I've never really played it because I don't like to run that much. But who knows? Maybe I'm a soccer genius.

Or maybe not. My first kick blops along the ground. The second one, I miss. The third one connects. The ball takes off and rattles the fence. Oh, yeah! I shake my fists and do a little jump. My winning goal will be like that.

"Whutcha doin?" a voice asks. I jump again. Aldeen Hummel, the Godzilla of Grade Three, is standing behind me. Where the heck did she come from?

"Um," I say, "playing soccer."

Aldeen squinches up her eyes behind her

smudgy glasses. Her witchy hair bounces.

"You should try it," I say, just to say something.

She puts her hands on her hips. "What for?"

Aldeen always makes me nervous, and when I get nervous, I blabber. I tell her all the stuff Charlie told me: the uniform you get, how everybody comes to watch and how you get a trophy after the tournament, plus the snacks and freezies.

"You should try it," I say.

Aldeen grunts and shuffles off. I figure I'm lucky. Sometimes when Aldeen gets bored she belts you. But I'm wrong about luck. And about being bored. When I go out for first practice, Aldeen Hummel is standing by the soccer balls.